청색의 / 별

KB193136

청색의 / 별

잠들기 전 한 문장의 위로,
비포슬립 필사집

당신의
모양

언제부터였을까요?

기억도 나지 않는 어린 시절부터 제 시선은

늘 주변 사람들의 얼굴을 향해 있었습니다.

그것은 제 눈에만 유독 도드라지는

표정 조각들 때문이었어요.

'아들 왔어?'라며 날 반기는

엄마의 밝은 미소 뒤에 걱정 한 조각,

'야, 이거 진짜 재밌지 않냐?'라며 낄낄거리는
친구의 웃음 뒤에 허무 한 조각.

짧게 떠올랐다 황급히 사라지는 그 표정들에
마음이 쓰였습니다.

그럴 때마다 저는 '무슨 일 있어? 얼굴이 왜 그래?' 하고
그들의 속을 물었어요.
같이 맛있는 음식을 먹으러 가거나
좋은 곳에 데리고 나가기도 했죠.

나의 작은 친절이 소중한 이의 심연까지
좋은 표정으로 만들 수 있기를 바라면서.

그러다 '고마워, 너랑 있으니까 괜찮아졌어'란 말을 들었을 때
뿌듯함을 넘어 감동 비슷한 걸 받았던 것 같아요.

내가 타인에게 도움이 되는 존재라는 사실,
그게 내 인생의 훈장이었어요.
그 이후로는 혹시나 힘든 사람들을 모르고 지나칠까
더욱더 주변의 얼굴을 살피며 살아온 것 같습니다.
그런데 이런 제 모습을 보고 한 친구가 말하더군요.

그게 바로 오지랖이 넓은 거라고.
너 그거 단점이야. 이렇게요.

그건 그냥 착한 아이 콤플렉스라고.
나의 인정 욕구 때문에 안 해도 될 행동들을 하는 거라고.
남들에게 이용만 당하고 네 실속은 못 챙기고 있다고.

사실은 나의 행동을 부담스러워하는 사람들이 많다고.
그런 단점들은 고쳐야 한다고.

'나의 이런 면이… 내 단점이었나?'

친구의 말은 충격적이었지만 맞는 것도 같았어요.
저도 가끔씩은 이런 제가 지칠 때도 있었으니까요.

그날 이후 저는 제 행동을
하나하나 다시 잡아보기 시작했습니다.

친구의 표정이 어두워 보이면
괜히 아는 척하는 게 부담될까 봐, 못 본 척 넘겼고

도움을 주고 싶은 상황이 생기면
내 마음 편하려는 행동이 아닐까, 그냥 두었고

누군가 제게 도움을 구하면 이 사람에게 내가 쉬워 보였나,
나를 돌아봤어요.

〈거절 잘하는 법〉, 〈스스로를 사랑하는 법〉 등
유튜브 인생 조언들을 찾아보면서
세상이 말하는 인생의 정답지대로 살고자 노력해 봤습니다.
그런데 왜일까요?

주변에 관심을 덜 주려는 노력만큼
확실히 내 시간은 더 많아졌지만
전 하나도 행복하지 않았어요.

단점을 고치면 내가 더 나은 사람이 될 줄 알았는데
단점을 고치기 위해 했던 행동들이
새로운 단점들을 줄줄이 만들어 내고 있던 거예요.

저는 의심 많고 예민하고 겁이 많은 사람이 되어갔고
스스로가 무엇 하나 마음에 드는 게 없었어요.

나는 어쩌다, 이 모양 이 꼴이 된 걸까?

그러던 어느 날, 1교시 수업이 있는 아침이었어요.

까딱하면 출석 체크를 놓칠 위기라
빠른 걸음으로 걷는 중에
자전거를 타는 한 꼬마 아이가 눈에 들어왔습니다.

자전거 타는 폼이 위태위태한 게
저러다 넘어질 것만 같아서
어느새 온 신경이 아이에게 집중됐는데
역시나, 커브를 돌던 아이가
옆으로 쿵, 쓰러져 버린 거예요.

저는 반사적으로 달려가 넘어진 아이를 일으켜 주었습니다.

"괜찮아? 많이 아팠지? 어디 다친 덴 없어?"
"네, 괜찮아요. 감사합니다."

그런데 괜찮다 말하는 아이의 말끝에서 순간,
불안 한 조각이 읽혔어요.
이 아이는 다시 자전거를 타기 겁내는 것 같았죠.

"많이 안 다쳐서 다행이다.
근데 너, 다시 자전거 타기 무섭지 않아?
어디 가는 길이었어? 데려다줄게."
"정말요? 감사합니다."

꾸벅 고개를 숙여 인사한 후 아이는 나를 보며
환한 미소를 지었어요.

저는 오래도록 그리워했던 표정을 만난 듯
마음 한구석이 뭉근하게 피어올랐습니다.

아이의 자전거를 끌고 아이 옆에 나란히 걸었어요.

어디 가는 길이었는지,

왜 혼자 가고 있었는지,

요즘은 뭐가 재미있는지,

내 직업은 뭐일 것 같은지,

시시콜콜한 대화를 주고받으며 걷다 보니

금방 꼬마의 초등학교 앞에 닿았습니다.

"잘 들어가~ 좋은 하루 보내!"

그새 친해진 아이와 아쉬운 작별 인사를 나누고

학교로 발걸음을 돌렸어요.

하지만 이미 시간은 1교시 전공 수업이 끝난 뒤였습니다.

또 실속 못 챙기고 남 좋은 일만 해줬다며
속 터져 하는 친구의 모습이 그려졌지만
문득 그런 생각이 들더라고요.

이렇게 행복한데 이게 정말 단점이라고 말할 수 있을까?
타인에겐 단점이어도 나에겐 장점이며
타인의 장점이 나에겐 단점일 수도 있는 거 아닐까?

적어도 나에게 이 단점은 장점이었어요.
어쩌면 장점과 단점은 같은 말이 아닐까 생각될 정도로.
오지랖 넓고 거절을 못 한다는 단점은
실은 배려심 많고 친절하다는 장점이고,

사소한 것에 집착한다는 단점은
실은 세심해서 실수가 적다는 장점이고,

감정 기복이 크고 예민하다는 단점은
실은 예술적 감수성이 풍부하다는 장점이고,

차분하지 못하고 정신 사납다는 단점은
실은 활동적이고 열정적이라는 장점이고,

매사에 부정적인 시각을 가졌다는 단점은
실은 더 나은 세상을 만드는 시선을 가졌다는
장점일 수 있어요.

장점과 단점을 굳이 나눌 필요가 있을까요?
그 모든 것들이 나의 모양이 되는데 말입니다.

나의 모든 결함은

곧 나를 가장 사랑스럽게 만드는 부분이에요.

있는 그대로의 내가 가장 자연스럽고 가장 아름답습니다.

당신의 모양은 어떤가요?

당신의 모서리가 누군가를 찌른다면,

조금 더 둥글게 다듬는 노력만으로도 괜찮아요.

당신의 모양을 망가뜨리지 마세요.

당신의 모양 그 자체로 완벽하게 예쁘니까요.

제가 이 모양 이 꼴 그대로

행복하듯 말이에요.

Monday

What Shape Are You in?

I'm not sure when it started.

But since some time in my childhood,
my gaze was always drawn to the faces of the people
around me.
It was the different looks on their faces
that seemed especially noticeable to my eyes.

The look of concern hidden behind my mother's bright

smile as she said,

"Oh, my son!"

The emptiness I saw behind

my friend's laughter as he giggled, saying,

"Bro, isn't this really hilarious?"

I was always aware of those fleeting expressions,

appearing only to quickly disappear from their faces.

Every time that happened, I would ask,

"Did something happen?

I can tell something's up from your face."

Then, I'd take them out to eat something delicious

or bring them somewhere nice,

hoping that my small kindness could brighten them up,

deep down, in the hearts of the ones dear to me.

When I'd hear,
"Thank you. You made me feel much better,"
It touched my heart in a way
that went beyond simple satisfaction.
The fact that I was someone who could help others.
That alone felt like a medal in my life.

Since then, I think I've lived my life paying
close attention to the faces around me,
just in case I might pass by someone struggling
through a rough patch.

But a friend of mine, who knows me well,

told me that I was a careholic.

And that it was my weakness.

And that it was just a good kid complex.

That I was doing things I didn't have to,

all because of my desire for recognition.

That I was letting myself be used by others

and failing to gain anything for my own good.

That, in fact, many people felt I was overbearing

because of my behavior.

That it was a weakness I needed to fix.

This side of me… was my weakness?

I was shocked to hear that from my friend.

But they seemed right, because sometimes,

I get tired of myself, too.

After that day, I started to reexamine my actions,

one by one.

When I saw a gloomy look on my friend's face,

I pretended not to notice it, afraid they might

find it burdensome that I did.

And when I felt the urge to help someone in need,

I held back, thinking it was probably just an act to make

myself feel good.

If someone asked too much of me,

I'd wonder if I somehow seemed easy to them.

I found myself searching for YouTube videos with titles

like *How to Say No* and *How to Love Yourself,*

trying to live according to what the world claims are

the right answers for life.

But how can I explain this?

The more I tried to care less about others,

the more time I had for myself.

But it didn't make me happy at all.

I thought that if I fixed this weakness,

I'd become a better person.

But instead, the actions I took to fix it only seemed

to create new weaknesses, one after another.

I became suspicious, sensitive, and fearful.

And I didn't like anything about myself.

How did I end up like this?

One morning, I was heading to my first class of the day.

I was walking briskly, eager not to miss

the attendance check,

when I noticed a little boy riding a bike.

He was riding so unsteadily

that I thought he might fall at any moment.

My attention locked onto him.

Sure enough, as he turned a corner,

he toppled over with a loud thud.

Without thinking, I ran over and helped him up.

"Are you okay? Does it hurt? Are you hurt anywhere?"

"No, I'm okay. Thank you."

But even as he said he was fine,

I caught a flicker of anxiety in his eyes.

The boy seemed scared to get back on the bike.

"I'm glad you're not hurt too badly.

But··· aren't you a little afraid to ride again?

Where were you headed? I'll walk you there."

"Really? Thank you."

The boy thanked me with a small bow and then gave me a

big, bright smile.

I felt a lump rise in my throat, as if I had just seen a look

I'd been longing to see for so long.

I walked alongside him, pulling his bike by my side.

We chatted about where he was going,

why he was riding alone, what kinds of things he enjoyed,

and even what he thought my job might be.

Before long, we arrived in front of his elementary school.

"Alright, off you go! Have fun today!"

Even though we'd only just met,

I felt a little sad to say goodbye.

But I left him and turned to head toward my own school.

By now, the first core class had already ended.

I pictured my friend giving me a hard time, nagging

that I'd helped someone else at the expense of my own responsibilities.

But I couldn't help but wonder.

"Can this really be a weakness if it makes me this happy?"

Could it be that what seems like a weakness to others is actually a strength to me?

And maybe, what other people see as a strength doesn't always feel that way to me?

At least for me, this weakness felt like a strength.

So much so, that I began to think maybe weaknesses and strengths might just be the same thing.

The weakness of being a careholic, of not being able to

say no, could actually be a strength

—of being considerate and kind.

The weakness of obsessing over trivial things

could be a strength

—of being meticulous and making fewer mistakes.

The weakness of being emotionally volatile

and sensitive could be a strength

—of being artistically in tune with the world.

The weakness of feeling restless

and mentally unstable could be a strength

—of being active and passionate.

The weakness of seeing things

through a negative lens could be a strength

—of having a perspective that pushes for a better world.

Is it really necessary to separate strengths from weaknesses?

When, in the end, I am the sum of them all?

Every one of my so-called weaknesses is

what makes me most lovable.

You are most natural, most beautiful,

when you are simply yourself.

What about you?

If your sharp edges poke someone,
that's okay.
Just try to soften them a little.

But don't ruin who you are.
Because you are perfectly beautiful,
just the way you are.

Just like I am happy, exactly the way I am.

파란
장미

열다섯의 봄…,
은은한 장미향이 우리를 감싼 그날.

아마 소풍이었을 거야.

고요했던 장미 정원은 우리 학교 아이들로 순식간에 소란한데
나의 귀에 너의 자리는 소리가 사라진 진공이었어.

교복을 입지 않은 너를 본 건 처음이었거든.

파란색 원피스를 입고 넌 장미향을 따라 걸었고
난, 너를 따라 걸었어.

"빨간 장미도 있고, 흰 장미도 있고, 분홍색 장미도 있는데
왜 파란 장미는 없을까?"

너는 내가 따라오는 걸 알았는지 갑자기 돌아보며 물었지.
나는 대답하지 못했어.

하지만, 마음속으로 말했어.

'네가 파란 장미인걸.'

너는 모르는 내 첫 번째 고백이었어.

열여덟의 여름…,
보슬비가 내렸던 어느 날,

비는 따뜻했고, 우리는 그 비를 함께 맞았지.
지쳐 보이는 너는 말했어.

"어떻게 살아야 할까?"

빗물 때문인지 너의 눈은 젖어 있었어.
닦아주고 싶었지만 내 손도 젖어 있었지.

"네가 무얼 하든 같이할게."

너에겐 첫 번째 고백처럼 들릴, 나의 두 번째 고백이었어.

점점 거세지는 빗줄기를 피해 우리는 그림을 그리며 놀았어.
넌 파란 장미를 그렸지.

"이 세상에 파란 장미는 없지만 꽃말은 있대.
파란 장미의 꽃말은 '불가능'이래."

그게 내 고백에 대한 너의 답인 걸 난 알았어.

스물의 가을…,
우리는 조금 자유로웠던 것 같아.
너는 너의 사랑을, 나는 나의 사랑을 찾아다녔지.

낙엽이 사그락 소리를 내며 밟히던 어느 맑은 날,
구름도 거의 없는 청아한 가을 하늘 아래,
우리는 앉아 있었어.

너는 너의 사랑과 헤어졌고,
난 나의 사랑과 헤어졌지.

너는 나를 이해하고,
나는 너를 이해하고.

그렇게 아무 말이 없는 대화를 나눴어.

스물여덟의 겨울…,
올해는 첫눈이 조금 늦었어.
하지만 첫눈답지 않은 함박눈이었지.

세상은 새하얗게 갓 내린 눈으로 덮였고
난 너에게 마지막 고백을 하고 싶었어.

파란 장미 꽃다발을 사서 너의 집으로 향했지.

우리가 열여덟일 때
파란 장미의 꽃말은 '불가능'이었지만
스물여덟의 우리에게 파란 장미의 꽃말은
'기적, 포기하지 않는 사랑'이래.

뽀득뽀득 눈길을 밟는 소리가 오늘따라 유난히 더 크게 들렸어.
너의 집 앞에 가까워지는 동안
파란 장미 위에도 하얀 눈이 앉았지.

아직 누구도 밟지 않은 하얀 눈길 위에서
떨리는 목소리로 너에게 전화를 걸었어.

"지금 너희 집 앞이야, 나와줄래?"

Tuesday

Seasons of First Love

We were fifteen. It was a spring day.

The scent of roses surrounded me.

We were probably on a class picnic.

The usually quiet rose garden buzzed

with the noise of our classmates.

But to my ears, where you stood was a silent vacuum.

Because it was the first time
I saw you without your school uniform.

You walked through the rose garden
in a blue dress, and I followed you.

"There are red roses, white roses, and pink roses···
but why aren't there blue roses?"

You asked, suddenly turning around,
as if you knew I was behind you.

I couldn't answer.

But in my mind, I whispered,

'You are a blue rose.'

That was my first confession.

The one you never heard.

We were eighteen. It was summer.

A light drizzle fell from the sky.

Looking tired, you said,

"How should I live now?"

Your eyes were wet, maybe from the rain.

I wanted to dry them, but my hands were wet too.

"I'll be there for you, whatever you do."

It was my second confession,
though it might have sounded like the first to you.

The rain grew heavier, and we passed the time sketching.

You drew a blue rose.

"There are no blue roses in the world,
but they still have a meaning.
The flower language of blue roses is *impossible*."

I knew that was your answer to my confession.

We were twenty. It was fall.

We seemed freer, somehow.

You searched for your love, and I searched for mine.

One clear day, with the rustling of fallen leaves beneath
our feet and the cloudless autumn sky stretched above,
we sat together.

You had broken up with your love,
and I had broken up with mine.
You understood me, and I understood you.

We had a conversation without saying a word.

We are twenty-eight. It was winter.

The first snow came late this year.

But when it did, the flakes were fluffy,

unusual for the season's first snowfall.

The world was blanketed in fresh white,

and I decided I would make my final confession to you.

I bought a bouquet of blue roses

and made my way to your house.

When we were eighteen,

blue roses meant *impossible*.

But at twenty-eight, they mean
miracle, a love that never gives up.

The sound of my footsteps on the snow-covered ground
echoed louder than usual.

As I neared your house, the white snow
began to settle on the blue petals.

I called you with a trembling voice,
standing on the untouched snow in front of your door.

"I'm in front of your house right now.
Will you come out?"

가뭄

내 마음이 메마르고 갈라져 폐허로 변하기 직전이었다는 것을
아마 그 누구도 알지 못할 것이다.

가만히 아무것도 하지 않고 아무것도 보지 않아도,
무언가를 열심히 하고 열심히 보아도,
처참하게 말라갔다.

마치 손바닥 위에 올린 마른 흙덩어리가
살짝 쥠에도 바스러지듯.

그렇게 바람에 쉽게 날려가듯.

겉은 멀쩡했다.
나는 모든 사람 앞에서 늘 그렇듯 잘 웃었고,
행복하다 말했다.

지금 사는 이 순간의 1분 1초가 너무나 소중하다고.
사실은 무엇이 소중한지
어떻게 소중히 대해야 할지 모른 채였다.

남들의 눈에 황폐한 밑천이 드러나는 건 죽기보다 싫어서
그저 괜찮다고 말하며 내가 할 수 있는 최선의
아무렇지 않음을 연기했다.

그렇게 겉과 속을 분리한 나는 쩌억 하니 갈라진
깊은 틈 사이에서 스스로 물 주는 법을 잊어갔다.

'뜨거운 물로 씻고 싶다. 씻고 싶은데. 씻어야 하는데…'

며칠째 이 생각을 하면서도 도무지 몸이 움직이지 않았다.

몇 시쯤 됐을까 시계를 보고 싶어
침대에 붙어버린 몸을 겨우 돌렸을 때,
집 안 한구석에 놓인 녀석이 눈에 들어왔다.
오랜 시간 꽤 공들여 키워온 아라리아 나무였다.

우연히 지나던 화원에서 첫눈에 반해 집으로 데려온
나의 유일한 반려 식물.

나는 이 아라리아 나무를 키우면서

식물 하나를 건사하기도 여간 힘든 게 아님을 배웠다.

4평 남짓한 이 공간에서

나를 제외한 유일한 생명체인 이 녀석을 잘 키워내고 싶었다.

일주일에 두 번, 물 주는 날을 정하고

내 애정의 크기만큼 듬뿍듬뿍 물을 주었다.

그리고 얼마 지나지 않아

아라리아는 시들어 가기 시작했다.

초보 식집사의 패착은 늘 무지성 애정이다.

부랴부랴 인터넷에 아라리아 살리는 법을 검색했다.

과습이 문제였다.

몇 날 며칠 나무에 물을 주지 않고 말려야 한다고 했다.

물을 주고 싶어서 몸이 근질거렸지만
꾹 참고 그대로 두었더니
아라리아의 이파리가 점점 생기를 되찾았다.

한 고비를 겨우 넘기자 또 다른 문제가 터졌는데
이번엔 햇빛이었다.

우리 집은 남향으로 볕이 잘 들었다.
그래서 겨우 종아리까지 오는 아라리아가
얼른 내 허리만큼, 키만큼 자라길 바라며
햇빛이 가장 내리쬐는 창가 자리에 녀석을 두었다.

그런데 이게 웬걸.
아라리아의 이파리는 어여쁜 녹갈색의 반짝임을 잃고
푸석한 갈색으로 변해갔다.

손으로 살짝 만지면
마른 나뭇잎 특유의 바스락거림이 느껴지더니
풍성했던 이파리가 우수수 떨어졌다.
해 몸살이었다.

다시금 인터넷 검색을 해보니 아라리아는
반그늘 아래서 잘 자라는 반음지식물이었다.
너무 강한 빛을 쬐어준 탓에 몸살을 앓은 것이다.

나는 정말 여러 번 이 녀석을 죽일 뻔했다.

초보 식집사의 패착은 역시나 무지성 애정이다.

나의 무수한 시행착오 속에서
생사의 고비를 넘겨온 아라리아는
그렇게 내 가족이 되었다.

이파리에 쌓인 먼지를 한 잎 한 잎 닦아주기도 하고
벌레가 생기면 약을 쳐주기도 하고,
추운 겨울에는 여름에나 쓰는 서큘레이터를 꺼내
바람을 쐬주기도 했다.
참 유난스러운 돌봄이었다.

아라리아는 내 노력을 알아주듯 쑥쑥 자라
어느새 내 허리만큼 키가 커졌다.

그렇게 애지중지 키워왔던 이 녀석을
언제 마지막으로 돌보았던가.

몸을 일으켜 아라리아 가까이 다가가 보았다.
바싹 마른 흙 위로
말라비틀어진 이파리들이 잔뜩 떨어져 있었다.

'꽤 아꼈는데, 너도 죽었구나…'

멍하니 녀석을 바라보다
'죽은 식물은 어떻게 버리지?'란 생각에 닿았다.
오랜 기간 '살리는 법'을 검색하던 내가,
'버리는 법'을 검색한다.

그런데 한 블로그에 이런 말이 쓰여 있었다.

죽은 식물을 무작정 버리기 전,

손톱으로 줄기를 살짝 긁어보세요.

줄기가 초록빛이라면 아직 살아 있는 거랍니다.

다시 사랑을 주며 키워보세요.

마른 잎이 다 떨어져도 금새 새잎이 예쁘게 핀답니다.

누가 봐도 죽은 나무였다.

그런데 살아 있을 수 있다고?

반신반의하며 손톱으로 아라리아 줄기를 살짝 긁어보았다.

긁힌 줄기 사이로 선명하게,

여린 빛의 초록색 속살이 드러났다.

나는 허리춤에 닿는 이 녀석을 위태위태하게 안아 들고는

곧바로 욕실로 향했다.

그리고 샤워기를 틀어 물을 주기 시작했다.
쏟아지는 물줄기에
그나마 말라붙어 있던 이파리 몇 개마저 모두 떨어졌지만,
녀석이 살아 있다는 믿음이 날 멈출 수 없게 했다.

아라리아는 흠뻑 젖었고,
어느새 나도 흠뻑 젖어 있었다.

욕실 한쪽에 아라리아를 두고 젖은 옷을 벗었다.

따뜻함을 넘어 뜨겁게 느껴지는 온도로 물을 맞추고
머리부터 발끝까지 골고루 떨어지도록 샤워기 물을 틀었다.

온몸을 타고 물이 흘러내렸다.

얼마만의 샤워인지 알 수 없어서 더욱 반가운 이 뜨거움.

그렇게 나에게 물을 주고 또 주었다.

욕실 안이 온통 뜨거운 김으로 가득 찰 때까지.

그렇게 나는 녀석과 다시 살아보기로 했다.

Drought

No one would have realized

that my heart was so parched and cracked,

teetering on the verge of turning into ruins.

Whether I sat still, doing nothing

and looking at nothing, or threw myself into work,

it kept parching, miserably.

Like a lump of dry soil crumbling

in the palm of your hand at the slightest touch.

Like dust, easily carried away by the wind.

On the outside, I was fine.

I smiled and told everyone I was happy,

just as I always did.

I said that every minute, every second of this life

I was living was precious.

But in truth, I didn't know what was precious

or how to cherish it.

I dreaded the thought of my desolate foundation

being exposed, so I kept saying I was okay.

I did my best to act as if nothing was wrong.

Separating my inside from my outside like that,

I eventually forgot how to water myself

—how to tend to the deep cracks

that had silently split open within me.

I want to wash with hot water.

I want to wash. I have to wash···

For days, my body didn't move at all as that thought

echoed in my mind.

When I finally peeled myself off the bed and turned to

glance at the clock, something in the corner of the room

caught my eye.

It was the aralia tree I had nurtured with so much care for
so long.

A plant I'd fallen in love with at first sight
in a flower shop I'd stumbled upon and brought home.
My only companion.

Raising that aralia tree taught me something:
even nurturing a single plant isn't easy.

I wanted to take good care of this little guy
—the only living thing in my tiny 13㎡ space.

I picked two days each week to water it and gave it
as much attention as I felt love for it.

But soon after, the aralia began to wither.

The mistake of a novice gardener is always
ignorant affection.

Panicked, I searched online for ways to save the aralia.
The problem was overwatering.

The advice was, I had to let the plant dry out
for a few days without giving it any water.
I itched with the urge to water it, but I held back.
Slowly, the aralia's leaves began to regain their vitality.

Just as I was overcoming one hurdle,

another problem appeared.

This time, it was sunlight.

My house faces south and gets plenty of sunshine.

So I placed the aralia, which barely reached my calves,

right in the sunniest spot by the window,

hoping it would quickly grow as tall as my waist.

But what the heck.

The aralia's leaves lost their beautiful green sheen

and turned a dull, lifeless brown.

When I touched them lightly,

I heard the rustling sound of brittle, dry leaves.

Then, the once-lush foliage fell away in clumps.

This time, the problem was too much sunlight.

Another internet search told me

that aralia trees grow best in semi-shade.

It had been suffering because I'd given it too much light.

I had almost killed this little guy several times.

The failure of a novice gardener, again,

was ignorant affection.

But the aralia, having survived these life-or-death crises

through my countless trials and errors,

became like family to me.

I wiped the dust off its leaves one by one,

and sprayed insecticide when bugs appeared.

In the cold winter,

I even pulled out the circulator

I normally only used in summer,

letting it gently air the plant.

It was extraordinary care.

The aralia grew quickly, as if it recognized my efforts.

Before I knew it, it had reached the height of my waist.

But when was the last time I had taken care of this plant

I had once nurtured so tenderly?

I got up and walked closer to it.

There were so many dried and twisted leaves

scattered across the parched soil.

I cared for you so much···

but you died too···.

I stared blankly at it, then wondered,

How do you dispose of a dead plant?

I had spent so long searching for *how to save*,

and now I found myself searching for *how to dispose*.

That's when I stumbled upon this on a blog.

Before you throw away a dead plant,
lightly scratch the stem with your fingernail.
If the stem is green, it's still alive.
Give it some love and nurture it again.
Even when all the dry leaves fall,
new ones will bloom beautifully.

It looked like a dead tree.
But··· could it still be alive?

Half in doubt, I scratched the aralia's stem
with my fingernail.

Between the scratched bark,

the delicate green flesh was clearly visible.

I cradled this fragile, waist-high plant

in my arms and carried it straight to the bathroom.

I turned on the shower and began to water it.

Even the few remaining leaves that had clung to

life fell away under the rushing water.

But the belief that it was alive didn't leave me.

I drenched the aralia, and before I knew it,

I was soaked too.

I placed the aralia carefully on one side of the bathroom,

then peeled off my wet clothes.

Turning the shower knob, I let the water run hot,

until it poured down, dripping evenly

from my head to my toes.

The water flowed down my entire body.

This warmth felt like a gift, because I didn't even know

how long it had been since I last showered.

I watered myself again and again,

until the bathroom was filled with hot steam.

That's how I decided to live—with this plant—again.

예쁜 이름표를
붙여주세요

난 사과를 좋아합니다.

풍부한 단맛과 적절히 새콤한 맛
그리고 입안에 가득 차는 과즙의 느낌을 사랑합니다.

사과 파이 속에서 뭉근하게 씹히는 달콤한 사과도 좋아합니다.
풀 향기가 나고 깨물면 '아삭' 하는 소리가 나는
파란 사과도 좋아합니다.

감자 샐러드 속에 숨어서 발견되기를 기다리고 있는
귀여운 사과도 좋아합니다.

가끔은 사과를 사러 마트에 나갑니다.
여러 가지 종류의 사과들이 쌓여 있습니다.

빨갛고 반짝이는 사과들을 지나면
한쪽 구석에 한 무리의 사과가 있습니다.

그 사과들에는 '못난이 사과'라고 이름표가 붙어 있습니다.
값도 아주 싸서 저 같은 사과 러버에게는
아주 고마운 존재입니다.

껍데기에 생채기가 조금 있기는 하지만
맛과 향기까지 다른 사과에 비해 뒤떨어지는 점은 없습니다.

이런 못난이 사과도 저는 사랑합니다.

그런데 이 사과들이 '못난이 사과'라고 불리는 게 전 싫습니다.
다른 마트에서는 이 사과들을 '알뜰 사과'라고 부릅니다.

이 이름도 전 싫습니다.
못난이는 아니지만 그 이름도 그냥 '싼 사과'일 뿐이잖아요.

이 사과들에게도 장점이 많은데, 겉모습 때문에
못난이라고 불리는 게 싫었어요.

그래서 예쁜 이름표를 붙여주고 싶어요.

사과에 이런 이름표가 붙어 있다면 어떨까요?

"겉모습은 터프하지만 달콤한 속내를 감추고 있는 사과."
"빨갛고 빛이 나서 사진 찍기 좋은 사과."
"과질이 부드러워서 잼 만들 때 최고의 사과."

혹은

"첫사랑의 풋풋함을 간직한 아삭하고 새콤한 사과."

어떤 사과에 손이 가나요?
사랑스럽지 않은 사과가 있나요?

간혹 우리는 스스로를 못난이 사과라고 불러요.

'난 소심해서 말을 제대로 못할 거야.'
이렇게 생각하고,
자기에게 '소심한 사람'이라는 이름표를 붙이죠.

그것보다는
"목소리는 작지만
귀 기울여 들을 만한 내용을 가지고 있는 사람"
이라고 이름표를 붙이는 게 어떨까요?

또 이렇게 자기를 생각하기도 합니다.
'난 결정을 못 해서 갈팡질팡하는 사람으로 보일 거야.'

그것보다는

"이것저것 경험해 보고 결론을 내는 창의적인 사람"

이라고 이름표를 붙이는 게 어떨까요?

우리는 어떤 사람을 이름표를 보고

'아~ 저 사람은 이런 사람이었구나' 하고 생각하게 된답니다.

나 자신도요.

그러니 나에게 예쁜 이름표를 붙여주세요.

나는 완벽하지 않아도 좋아요.

완벽이란 없으니까요.

나의 아픔과 기쁨을 떠올려 보세요.

나를 찾고 안아주고 이야기를 들어주세요.

그러니까 나에게 예쁜 이름표를 붙여주려면
나를 사랑해야 한다는 얘기예요.
내가 사과를 사랑해서 예쁜 이름표를 붙여주었듯이 말이죠.

눈뜨기 힘든 아침에도 이불을 박차고 나오는,
용기 있는 나를 사랑합니다.

택배 아저씨랑 엘리베이터를 탈 때 문을 잡아주는,
친절한 나를 사랑합니다.

책을 읽다가 소파에서 잠시 잠드는,
여유 있는 나를 사랑합니다.

왼발 다음에 오른발을 내뻗어 걸을 만큼,
성실한 나를 사랑합니다.

다른 사람이 생각하는 내가 아니라
지금 이대로의 나에게 예쁜 이름표를 붙이고
다정하게 불러주세요.

아! 아무 이름표도 떠오르지 않아도 괜찮아요.
이렇게 해보세요.

"이름표를 고민하는 나를 사랑합니다."
"지금 여기에 있는 나를 사랑합니다."
"나를 사랑하는 나를 사랑합니다."

Pieces of Me,
Loved Completely

I love apples.

I love their rich sweetness,
the perfect hint of tartness,
and that juicy burst that fills my mouth.

I love the sweet, tender apples
that turn soft and mushy inside an apple pie.

I love the crisp, green apples
that smell like freshly cut grass.

I love the little chunks of apple hiding in potato salad,
waiting to be discovered.

Sometimes, I go to the market just to buy apples.
There are piles and piles of different kinds of apples.

As I walk past the bright, red, shiny ones,
I always notice a bunch of apples
tucked away in one corner.

They're labeled 'ugly apples.'

They're also much cheaper,
which makes them a great find for an apple lover like me.

Even though their skins are a little bruised or scratched,
they're just as delicious and fragrant as any other apple.

I love these "ugly" apples too.

But I hate that they're called 'ugly apples.'

Some markets try to be nicer and call them 'frugal apples.'
But I hate that name, too.

It's not ugly, sure, but it still feels like
they're just being called "cheap apples."

These apples are wonderful in so many ways,
and I don't like that people judge them
just because of how they look.

That's why I want to give them pretty names.

What if apples had names like these?

"An apple that looks tough on the outside,
but is sweet on the inside."
"A red, shiny apple that's perfect for photos."
"An apple with a soft texture, perfect for making jam."

Or even,

"A crunchy, sour apple

that captures the freshness of first love."

Which apple are you drawn to?

Is there an apple you don't find lovely?

Sometimes, we call ourselves ugly apples.

Someone might think,

"I'm shy and won't be able to speak properly,"

and label themselves as 'a shy person.'

But what about "a person with a quiet voice
but something worth listening to"?

Another might think,
"People see me as indecisive, unstable."

But what about
"a creative soul who explores different paths
before finding the right one"?

We tend to accept people's labels and think,
"Oh, that's just the way they are."

I do that too.

But what if you gave yourself a prettier label?

It's okay if you're not perfect.

Because there's no such thing as perfection.

Think about your pain and your joy.

Find yourself, hold yourself close,

and listen to your own story.

That means, to give yourself a beautiful label,

you first need to love yourself.

Just like I gave those apples pretty names

because I love apples.

I love the courageous me

who kicks off the blanket and gets out of bed,

even on mornings when it feels impossible

to open my eyes.

I love the kind me

who holds the elevator door open for the delivery person.

I love the carefree me

who reads a book and dozes off on the couch.

I love the sincere me

who takes one step after another, right foot after left.

Instead of focusing on what others think of you,

give yourself a beautiful label

and call yourself with affection.

Ah! It's okay if you can't think of a label right now.

It can be something as simple as:

"I love the me who's thinking about my label."

"I love the me who's here, right now."

"I love the me who's learning to love myself."

I'm BLUE

오랜만에 본가 가족들을 만났어요.
제 생일이었거든요.

늘 그렇듯 엄마는 상다리가 부러지도록
진수성찬을 차려주셨고,
배가 넘치게 부른데도 더 먹으라는 엄마의 성화에
억지로 몇 입 더 입에 넣었죠.

"우리 아들은 역시 엄마 말 잘 듣는 순둥이라니까.
사춘기도 없었던 예쁜 아들. 너무 착하게 잘 자라줘서
엄마가 너무 고마워. 우리 아들 최고!"

장난스럽게 엄지를 흔들며 웃는 엄마를 보면서
나도 웃음이 났지만,
저라고 왜 사춘기가 없었겠어요.

중학생인 나에게도 엄마 아빠의 고된 삶이 눈에 보여
그저 조용히 지내왔을 뿐인 것을.

저의 사춘기도 누구나의 사춘기처럼 우울했습니다.

점점 굵고 낮아지는 목소리가 스스로도 낯설었던 시기.

마냥 즐겁고 모든 게 신났던 어릴 적과는 다르게

하나둘 공부할 거리가 늘어나고,

나중에 무엇을 하고 싶은지,

나는 뭘 좋아하는 사람인지도 모르는데

어딜 가든 '넌 꿈이 뭐니? 어떤 사람이 되고 싶니?'를

물어오는 게 부담스럽다는 생각을 하곤 했어요.

무엇보다 내가 중심인 세상에서 세상 속의 나로

관점이 이동하면서

집안 형편상,

내가 욕심내선 안 되는 것들이 보이기 시작했고

시작도 하기 전에 지레 포기하는 게 점점 많아졌습니다.

여러 가지가 마구잡이로 엉킨

나쁜 감정 덩어리는 옷 속에 꽁꽁 감춰져

나만 볼 수 있는 퍼런 멍 같았어요.

누구에게도 말하기 싫고 들켜서도 안 되는 못난 마음이었죠.

결코 내보이고 싶지 않은 나만의 우울.

우울은 점점 더 탁하고 시퍼렇게 내 몸에 번져 나갔어요.

엄마는 아직도 모르시지만,

가출을 감행한 날이 있었어요.

도저히 책상에 앉아 있을 수도 없고

그렇다고 누구와 대화하고 싶지도 않은,

이러지도 저러지도 못하겠는데

뭐라도 해야겠는 그런 날 있잖아요.

"시험 기간이라 독서실에서 공부하고 늦게 들어올게."
엄마에게 거짓말을 하고 고속버스 터미널로 향했어요.

엄마와 외할머니 집에 내려갈 때 몇 번 와본 적은 있었지만
혼자서는 처음이어서 행여나 잘못 탈까
번호를 몇 번씩 확인하고 버스에 올랐죠.

버스 안에서 보이는 풍경이 네모난 건물들에서
논밭으로 바뀌고도 한참을 달렸어요.

저의 목적지는 천체관측소.

매표소 앞에는 홀로 이곳에 온 저와 천문 동아리에서 온
타 학교 친구들이 있었어요.

호기롭게 가출을 했지만 내심 무섭기도 했는데
매표소 앞의 다른 학교 선생님을 보자 안심이 되었던 걸 보면
역시나 아이는 아이였던 것 같네요.
천문 동아리 친구들 사이에 섞여서
어두컴컴한 산꼭대기를 걸어 올랐습니다.

숨이 살짝 찰 즈음 천체관측소에 닿았어요.

눈앞에 놓인 돔의 웅장함에 압도되자마자
변신 로봇처럼 돔의 지붕이 열렸고
'와아—' 하고 친구들의 탄성이 터졌습니다.

저는 차마 입을 열지는 못했고
속으로만 '와아~ 멋지다' 하고 기뻐했었죠.

거대한 천체관측 망원경에 눈을 대고 밤하늘의 별을
바라보았어요.

제가 처음 봤던 별은 비너스.
금성이었어요.

맨눈으로 보았을 때는 그저 반짝이는 점 같았던 별이
망원경으로 보니 마치 사막의 모래를
동그랗게 뭉쳐놓은 것처럼 보였어요.

내내 조용히 닫혀 있던 제 입에서도
작게 '우와' 소리가 새어 나왔죠.

그때 한 친구가 이런 질문을 했어요.

"선생님, 금성이 가장 뜨거운 별 맞죠?"

선생님이 말씀하셨어요.

"아니, 사실 금성은 그리 뜨겁지 않은 별이야.
최근에 과학자들이 우주에서 가장 뜨거운 별을 찾았지.
여기서 문제! 그 별이 무슨 색인지 아는 사람?"

천문 동아리 친구들이 너도나도 손을 들며 외쳤어요.

"빨간색이요!"
"노란색!"
"주황색!"

저는 열띤 친구들 사이에서
속으로 '빨간색!'을 외치며 선생님을 바라보았어요.

선생님은 고개를 가로저으며 말씀하셨어요.

"아니야. 완벽한 파란색이란다."

예상을 빗나간 답변에 친구들은 웅성거렸고,
저는 더욱 호기심이 일었어요.

"우리가 밤하늘을 올려다보면,
별들은 모두 반짝이는 하얀색으로 보이지?
하지만 저 별들 모두가 각기 다른 색을 가지고 있지.
그리고 그 색에 따라서 온도가 제각각이란다.

빨간 별보다 노란 별이,

노란 별보다는 파란 별이 더 뜨거워.

청색의 별은 가장 파랗지만

가장 뜨겁게 타오르는 별이야."

제 인생에 가장 큰 일탈이었던 그날의 밤.

아무 일도 없었다는 듯 집에 돌아온 나는

천문 동아리 선생님이 말씀하셨던

파란 별에 대해 알아봤어요.

그 별의 이름은

백색왜성 RX J0439.8-6809

강렬한 푸른빛을 내뿜는 아름다운 별이었어요.

심지어 태양보다 42배 뜨거운.

I'm BLUE.

더 이상 이 문장이 전처럼

우울하게 느껴지지 않았어요.

강인하고 아름다운 파랑이 바로 나니까.

퍼렇게 나를 덮었던 멍 자국들은

살짝만 건드려도 아팠지만,

그때의 성장통이 지금의 성숙한 나를 만든 것 같아요.

어른이 된 내가 소년인 나를 만날 수 있다면
이 말을 꼭 전해주고 싶어요.

"BLUE is a Piece of Life."
"BLUE is Beautiful and Sad."

"You're in BLUE paradise."

I'm BLUE

I went to my parents' house after a long time.

It was my birthday.

As always, my mom cooked up a storm in the kitchen,

preparing a feast just for me.

I was already full,

but she kept insisting I eat more,

so I shoved a few extra bites into my mouth.

"My son is such a sweet boy

who listens to his mom so well.

My sweet son never even went through puberty.

I'm so grateful to you for growing up so well

and being so good. My son is the best!"

She playfully gave me a thumbs-up with a big smile,

and I couldn't help but smile back.

But she's wrong. I did go through puberty.

Back then, in middle school,

I could already see how much

my parents were struggling.

So I kept everything to myself.

In my puberty, I was blue, just like everyone else.

My voice was getting heavier, lower,
and even that felt awkward to me.

When I was little, I was always happy and excited.
But as I grew up, the things I had to study piled up.

I didn't even know what I wanted to do
in the future or what I really liked,
but people always asked,

"What's your dream?
What kind of person do you want to be?"
Those questions weighed on me.

I used to feel like the center of my world.

But at some point, I realized I was just a small part of it.

With that shift, I started noticing things

I wanted but knew my family couldn't afford.

And slowly, I began giving up on things

before I even had a chance to start.

A mess of bad emotions tangled up inside me,

like a blue bruise only I could see,

hidden tightly under my clothes.

It was a shameful feeling,

one I didn't want to tell anyone about.

Something I didn't want anyone to catch.

My own blue that I never wanted to show.

My blue spread, deeper and murkier,

until it filled my whole body.

My mom still doesn't know,

but there was a day when I tried to run away from home.

You know those days when you just can't sit at your desk,

don't want to talk to anyone,

but still feel like you have to do something?

"It's exam period. I'll study in the library
and come home late,"
I lied to my mom, grabbing my bag
and heading straight to the express bus terminal.

I'd been there a few times before
when I traveled to my grandma's house with my mom.

But this was my first time going alone,
and I couldn't shake the worry
that I might get on the wrong bus.
I double-checked the bus number,
then checked it again.
Finally, I got on.

As the bus pulled away,

the scenery outside shifted from square buildings

and crowded streets to wide-open rice paddies

and empty fields.

The bus rumbled on for a long time.

My destination was the observatory.

In front of the ticket booth were me

and friends from another school's astronomy club.

I had bravely run away, but I was also a little scared.

Then I spotted their teacher standing

by the ticket booth, and I felt relieved.

I guess··· I was still just a kid.

I hiked up the dark mountain with them,

out of breath by the time we reached the observatory.

I was overwhelmed by the towering dome

as its roof began to open,

shifting like a transforming robot.

"Wow!" they all gasped in unison.

I couldn't bring myself to say anything out loud,

but inside, I was shouting,

'Wow, this is amazing.'

Then, I looked up at the stars

  through the enormous astronomical telescope.

The first star I saw was the morning star.

It was Venus.

To the naked eye,

the star was just a tiny dot of light,

but through the telescope,

it looked like a round ball of desert sand.

I'd been quiet the whole time,

but at that sight,

a small "wow" escaped from my lips.

Then, one of the students asked the teacher,

"Teacher, Venus is the hottest star, right?"

The teacher replied,
"Not really. Venus isn't really hot.
Scientists have recently discovered
the hottest star in the universe.
Here's a question for you!
Does anyone know what color that star is?"

Students from the astronomy club

eagerly shouted out answers.

"Red!"

"Yellow!"

"Orange!"

Caught up in their excitement,

I said "Red!" to myself and looked at the teacher.

But the teacher shook his head and said,

"No. It's a perfect blue."

The group fell into a quiet murmur,

surprised by the unexpected answer.

I felt a sudden surge of curiosity.

"When we look up at the night sky,
all the stars seem like they're twinkling white, right?
But in reality, each of those stars has its own color.
And each color tells us something
about the star's temperature.

Yellow stars are hotter than red stars,
and blue stars are hotter than yellow stars.
Blue stars are the bluest,
but they burn the hottest."

That night was the biggest deviation of my life.

I returned home as if nothing had happened.

Curious, I looked up the blue star

the astronomy club teacher had mentioned.

The star's name was White Dwarf RX J0439.8-6809.

It was a beautiful star,

radiating an intense blue light.

And it was 42 times hotter than the sun.

I'm BLUE.

But this sentence doesn't feel

as heavy or depressing as it once did.

Because now, I am the strong and beautiful blue.

Tender bruises that hurt with even the slightest
touch had once covered me in blue.

Those growing pains shaped me
into the person I am today.

I'm an adult now.
But if I could meet my teenage self,

I really want to say
"BLUE is a Piece of life."
"BLUE is Beautiful and Sad."
"You're in a BLUE paradise."

청색의 별

dingo story 글 채령 · 수 · 키하노 글도움 Guihwa H. Blanz 영어 번역
초판 1쇄 발행일 2025년 4월 25일
펴낸이 이숙진 펴낸곳 (주)크레용하우스 출판등록 제1998-000024호
주소 서울 광진구 천호대로 709-9 전화 (02)3436-1711 팩스 (02)3436-1410
인스타그램 @bizn_books 이메일 crayon@crayonhouse.co.kr

＊빚은책들은 재미와 가치가 공존하는 ㈜크레용하우스의 도서 브랜드입니다.

ISBN 979-11-7121-166-1 04810